JESSICA THE WIZARD
EATS A THIRD HORSE

A Novelette By

JASON STEELE

For the horses forgotten.

"The wagon rests in winter, the sleigh in summer, the horse never."
~ YIDDISH PROVERB

CHAPTER ONE

The World of Magical Investments

A tall, translucent blob wearing a mass of clumpy orange robes sped across a vast and dreary office, ignoring the disapproving looks of the various business casual wizards it was nearly running into. The strange, viscous figure twisted its gooey head from side to side, observing everything it could as it whizzed past gray filing cabinets and empty gray meeting rooms.

The blob began to slow, and then stopped altogether in front of a large wooden door with a brass nameplate reading, "Jessica Magic." A long, translucent tendril emerged from the orange robes and pressed itself into a glowing rune on the door, which had been carved where a doorknob would typically be.

The door vanished in a puff of smoke, revealing a small, modern office filled with vaguely magical-looking office items. A black fax machine floated above the room's only desk, and a large calculator slowly inched itself across the gray checkered carpet.

As the blob entered the room it became less and less translucent, and less and less blobish, until standing in its place was a tall woman with raven-black hair and striking, lizard-like facial features. She removed her orange robe, revealing a smaller, more business-like robe underneath, which was also orange.

"Let's hope things work out this time," said the woman, making her way to the desk at the other end of the room. She took care to step over the calculator, which had briefly halted its journey to watch her cross. "It's hard enough getting a job with a past like mine, let alone a job at a magical investment firm."

"Did you say something?" asked a man who was walking by the room, his gangly arms clutching a large stack of dull-looking documents and scans of those same documents.

"Yes," replied the orange-robed woman, sitting herself down in an egg-shaped chair at the desk. "I said a lot of things. Don't worry about it."

"Okay."

The man left, looking as though he was not in fact worrying about it. The woman waved her hand and the door to the office re-appeared, sealing the room off from the rest of the building. The calculator on the floor was inching along again, at a faster pace than before.

"If this job doesn't work out I don't know what I'm going to do," the woman said, very loudly, to herself. She reached into her robe and pulled out a small, orange business card. On it were the words, "JESSICA MAGIC: MAGICAL INVESTMENTS."

"That's me," said Jessica, putting the card down on her desk. "I guess I'm a magical investor now." She sighed deeply, a sigh filled with the resonance of her many regrets.

Jessica had experienced a lot in her 30 years of wizarding life, but much of it she would rather forget. For instance, she had eaten two entire living horses. She just swallowed them up in one huge, magical bite. Not both at the same time, mind you—the horse eatings occurred a few years apart. But it was a thing that had happened, and it was a thing she hated herself for.

"Knock knock," boomed a voice from outside the door. "I would knock for real, but these are illusory doors and knocking doesn't work on them."

"Come in," said Jessica. She focused her gaze intensely on the door, so that she could stare whoever was entering directly in the eyes from the very first moment they entered. It was a wizard power move.

The door vanished, and in walked Dr. Clash, president of the company and Jessica's new boss. Dr. Clash was, impressively, staring at exactly the spot where Jessica's eyes were, unreservedly winning the power dynamic.

Dr. Clash was an intense-looking woman with sword-silver hair and a sharp, swordly-chin. The sleeves of her navy blue pantsuit had been carefully tailored off to showcase her huge, bulging wizard arms—the biggest Jessica had ever seen. Jessica was no wimp herself, mind you, but her two hundred push-ups a day could not compete with the superior muscle-magic that Dr. Clash had going on.

"You must be Jessica," said Dr. Clash as she thumped

forward. "Welcome to Magical Investments. I'm Dr. Clash, I run the day-to-day operations here." Dr. Clash held out her hand for a handshake, which Jessica gladly accepted.

"What a grip," said Jessica, out loud. "I cannot believe your arms, they're amazing. I'm sorry if that's an unprofessional thing to say, but good god Dr. Clash, *those arms…*"

"I'm caught in a magical time loop. At the end of each day I get transported to another realm for around forty hours. There's nothing there but rocks and boulders, so I just lift stuff until I'm sent back into this reality."

"I've eaten two whole horses," replied Jessica, without thinking. Her hand shot up and cupped her mouth. "Oh my god, I can't believe I just told you that. I've never told anyone."

It was true, Jessica had never told anyone about her horse eating. But there was something about Dr. Clash that made Jessica feel like she could tell her anything, without judgement.

"Don't worry about it. As long as you do good, uh, *investment work,* and don't eat any horses on the job, you'll do fine here." Dr. Clash put her gigantic hands on Jessica's shoulders. "If you need anything, my office is on the top floor, in the wizard spire."

"Okay, yes, I will definitely stop by your wizard spire sometime."

"Excellent. Well, may your magic be bold and your numbers bolder. Or whatever our company motto is." With that, Dr. Clash gave a stately salute, turned around, and swaggered out of the room.

"If those arms were a horse I would eat them," said Jessica.

"What?" asked the man from earlier, walking by the room again. "Were you talking to me?"

"No. Who are you even?" Jessica waved the door shut before he could answer.

CHAPTER TWO

The Dark Wizard

Jessica spent the majority of her first week at Magical Investments learning how to use the magical office equipment. Her assumption was that the charms the equipment had been imbued with would make them more efficient than their regular, non-magical counterparts. She soon discovered, however, that the magic they possessed simply made them more rebellious and unruly.

Her fax machine, for instance, was by most accounts a normal fax machine. Except instead of sitting in one place on her desk it would float around on its own, slowly knocking over other equipment until she would give in and find something to fax. The kitchen coffee maker was much the same story—when it ran out of coffee it would float around the office knocking over any non-coffee beverages until a fresh pot was brewed.

The copy machine was the worst of all. It would, on occasion, make an exact physical duplicate of the entire office staff and then violently destroy them in front of whomever happened to be near. So, if you needed something copied you had to mentally prepare yourself for the possibility of witnessing the horrific death of yourself and your co-workers.

The only piece of magical equipment that Jessica actually appreciated was her huge black desk phone, which whispered demonic prophecies in her ear as she made important business calls. The calls were unbearably dull otherwise, and she figured it was better to be informed about the plans of hell than to be taken by surprise.

* * *

It was just about lunchtime on her sixth day when Jessica heard a noise she didn't recognize. The noise was chunky and high-pitched, like a laser-beam cutting through a suitcase full of fish. Ten seconds later it stopped, and there was a faint pop, at which point the lights in her office dimmed.

The phone on Jessica's desk rang, and the lights in her office dimmed even further. She hesitated for a moment, and then cautiously picked up the phone and held it to her ear. The office lights began flickered ominously.

"Jessica, I need to see you in my wizard spire immediately." It was the voice of Dr. Clash, her speech barely audible over the ramblings of a demon muttering nonsense about a cavern filled with ancient gray blood.

"I'll be right there." As Jessica hung up the phone, she felt a knot tightening in her stomach. She wasn't sure how, but deep within her wizard soul she knew: the events to follow would culminate in her eating an entire third live horse.

* * *

Dr. Clash's office wasn't at all what Jessica had expected. It was delicate, and elegant in an old-fashioned sort of way. A beautiful porcelain tea set sat on a small oak table next to a window that overlooked the city. A sofa, that looked to Jessica a lot like a fainting couch, was positioned in the center of the room on top of an ornate red and gold rug.

"Please, have a seat," said Dr. Clash, motioning to the couch. Jessica pretended to faint dramatically on it, but Dr. Clash didn't notice. Feeling embarrassed, Jessica sat up and tried to look as professional as possible.

Dr. Clash was nervously wringing her enormous hands together and pacing around the room. Each step sent a small tremor through the furniture, and Jessica could hear the porcelain tea set rattling ever so slightly. There was something about feeling the vibration of Dr. Clash's steps that comforted Jessica, even though the pacing itself made her uneasy.

After a few moments Dr. Clash stopped pacing, and looked toward Jessica. "All of our money has been stolen," she said.

"What?" Jessica tried to sound as unsuspicious as possible, even though she had nothing to do with the stolen money.

"A few minutes ago a very powerful wizard broke into our vault and teleported all of our wizard gold away."

"Oh my god. I didn't even realize we kept wizard gold

here." Jessica was still trying really hard to sound like she had nothing to do with the robbery.

"Only the board of directors and myself know. Magical Investments is not just an investment firm, it's also a sort of hub for wizard market transfers." Dr. Clash walked over to the tea pot and began pouring some tea. "Half of all wizard gold traded on the wizard market ends up here."

"I really had no idea," said Jessica, realizing that everything she was saying sounded more and more suspicious.

"Tea?" Dr. Clash handed a red and gold porcelain tea cup to Jessica. The smell of chai pleasantly wafted from it.

"Thank you." Jessica sipped from the cup. She didn't much care for chai, but it was very well prepared tea. "Do you have any idea who could be behind the robbery?"

Dr. Clash began pacing again, carefully drinking from her cup. It occurred to Jessica that she looked a bit like a cultured rhinoceros.

"I believe it was someone on our board of directors," said Dr. Clash. Her pacing slowed. "Our newest board member is a dark wizard named Sacrifice, known for her extremely powerful teleportation skills."

"We have dark wizards on our board of directors?"

Dr. Clash looked soberly at Jessica. "The world of wizard finance is filled with dark wizards."

Jessica looked away from Dr. Clash, embarrassed to have asked such a naive question. "So, what did you need from me?"

For a moment Dr. Clash simply stared at Jessica, as if trying to solve a wizard puzzle cube. Then, she waved her hand and a thick manila folder appeared in it. "Here's everything I have on Sacrifice. I want you to investigate her. I would go to the wizard police, but I don't want our clients knowing about this if they don't have to."

Jessica set her cup down on the floor and grabbed the folder. Bits of light sparked out of it, and there was a faint smell of burning powder. It was definitely a magical folder.

"Why me?" asked Jessica, trying not to let any papers crawl out of the folder. "Surely there are people better qualified for this task."

"I haven't been completely honest with you, Jessica." Dr. Clash walked over to the tea pot and poured herself another cup. "I didn't hire you for your investment skills. I hired you because of your experience with dark wizards."

It was true, Jessica had interacted with an absurd number of dark wizards, even killed some of them. She didn't have any particular dislike of them, in fact her own ethical code was closer to that of dark wizards than to the wizards of the light. But she was very good at challenging them and surviving, and the opportunity to do so had arisen many times during her life.

"I see. I was wondering how I got this job with, like, zero financial experience. I suspected something was up, but I didn't think it would be this."

"I'm sorry for not being upfront with you. I'm still not being completely upfront with you, but this is all I can reveal at the moment. Too much is at stake."

Dr. Clash drank the rest of her tea and set the empty cup on the table next to the pot. She stared at the pot for a moment, and then looked over at Jessica.

"I don't want you to kill her. I just want you to find out if she took the gold. And please, this assignment is between you and me. Do not talk to anyone on the board of directors about this. Can you do that?"

Jessica stood up, clasping the magical folder tightly under her arms. "I'll do everything I can, Dr. Clash." As she said that, an image flashed inside Jessica's mind of a large, majestic horse spiraling helplessly into the cavernous abyss of her mouth.

CHAPTER THREE

Magical Investigations

The financial capital of the wizarding world was, indisputably, Bloodfist City. Most of the largest wizarding banks had their headquarters there, and the largest magical stock market in the world was located in the very center of the city's business district. It was a sprawling, modern city, surrounded on all sides by barren, oppressive deserts.

On the far southern edge of the city sat a long street full of tall, twisted apartment buildings. They were ancient wizarding towers that had been around for centuries, converted into living spaces and updated with modern conveniences like magical plumbing and magical slime disposal. On the very top floor of the twistiest building was a group of studio apartments, and it was in one of those apartments that Jessica lived.

Moving boxes filled with her things were stacked against the far wall, blocking the apartment's only window, and in the middle of the room was a bed covered in clothes and paperwork. Except for being untidy, her apartment was very clean and had a warm, sturdy quality about it.

Every night when Jessica came home she would throw her clothes onto the clothes pile, and make herself a cup of instant wizard noodles. The noodles were salty and satisfying, but you had to eat them quickly or else they would vanish, only to re-appear later at an unfortunate time and place.

After eating she would do two hundred push-ups and then fall asleep under the pile of clothes on her bed. It wasn't a routine she was happy with, but it was the routine she was stuck in. Tonight, however, she had a reason to stay awake, to keep herself far away from her recurring horse-eating dreams. Tonight she had research to do.

She opened the manilla folder Dr. Clash had given her, careful to prevent any of the magical papers inside from getting away. The first page was a black and white photograph of a woman, titled, "Board Member Portrait: Sacrifice." Jessica lifted the photo and studied it closely. Sacrifice had dark, short hair that spiked up like daggers, and pitch-black eyes surrounded by dark, messy eyeshadow. She was wearing a studded leather jacket with a leopard-print inlay, and around her neck hung a small pendant with dangerous looking runes on it.

"She looks rad," Jessica said to herself, and then nodded approvingly.

The rest of the papers in the folder were police reports and newspaper articles about various dark crimes that Sacrifice had committed, as well as a press release by Magical Investments stating that they had added Sacrifice to their board of directors to *"… strengthen our alternative financial strategies."*

There wasn't much to go on. Sacrifice was clearly a capable dark wizard with a long criminal history, but that didn't mean she had committed this specific crime.

"I want more noodles." Jessica got up and made another cup of wizard noodles. As she did, the various papers in the manilla folder began creeping around her apartment like flat white snakes. The portrait slowly inched its way up a wall, Sacrifice's dark eyes gazing coldly at Jessica.

An old memory began rattling around inside Jessica's head. A memory of a spell, taught to her by the dark wizard Fire Tiara, to summon the essence of another wizard for a short period of time. It was a difficult spell to cast, and not particularly useful. You weren't really summoning someone, just an abstraction of them, a ripple of their existence. But Jessica didn't have any other ideas.

She set down her half-eaten noodles and walked over to one of the moving boxes that was stacked against the wall. Inside the box was various enchanted items and ingredients, which began shaking with excitement at the prospect of finally being utilized. Jessica grabbed a small purple bottle, and a red feather that was tucked inside a tiny cloth sleeve. As she closed the box, the unchosen objects made a faint, disappointed sigh.

The photograph of Sacrifice was now most of the way up the wall, and it took a few good jumps before Jessica was able to grab it down. She opened the purple bottle and dipped the feather in, at which point the bottle began twitching around in her hands. The shaft of the feather was now covered in a strange, sparkling purple substance, which Jessica was careful to not let drip anywhere except back into the bottle. As soon as the dripping stopped she slowly moved the feather over to the photograph, and with very clear handwriting wrote four words across Sacrifice's face: "Hey, come over here."

The photograph twitched and shook, and emitted a terrible high-pitched howl. Unfazed, Jessica hurriedly put the cap back on the bottle and tucked the feather into its sleeve. The howling stopped, and the photograph burst into a purple flame. A thick, white plume of smoke rose from the fire and formed itself into the shape of Sacrifice. Jessica instinctively took a step back—even through the vagueness of the smoke, Sacrifice was an imposing figure.

"Who are you, and why have you summoned me?" boomed the voice of Sacrifice from out of the smoke, rattling the walls and causing Jessica to take a second quick step back.

"Uhh…" This was not what Jessica was expecting to hear from the essence of Sacrifice, as wizard essences were usually ethereal and docile. "My name is Jessica. I wanted to ask you a few questions."

"I'm taking a shower right now. Do you realize that? I'm standing in my shower."

Jessica paused, perplexed. "How are you taking a shower?"

"What? How am I… what?" Sacrifice's face twisted. "Again, why have you summoned me?

"I wanted to ask you a few questions, about Magical Investments."

"I can't talk about that. Can't and won't. Also, I'm showering."

Jessica could not believe what she was hearing. "Uh, you have to answer me. You're not supposed to be able to not answer me."

Sacrifice's face twisted even further, and then morphed into a wicked smile. "Hmm, okay, uh, Jessica, what spell do you think you're casting?"

Jessica felt as though she had been shot with an arrow. Her mind began racing through the different summoning spells Fire Tiara had taught her.

"Oh god," said Jessica, covering her mouth with both her hands. "I opened a talk-way. You're actually Sacrifice."

"If you wanted to summon my essence you needed one of my possessions, not a photograph."

"Yeah. Yeah that was it." Jessica sat down and put her hands over her head. "Grrruuuhhhhhhhh I can't believe I've done this."

"Well, you did a great job casting it, even if it was the wrong spell. This is the clearest talk-way I've been on in a while."

"Thanks." Jessica began rolling around on the ground in embarrassment.

"Of course, because you cast it so well we're going to be stuck in this call for, like, twenty minutes."

"Yeah. Sorry about that. Sorry for interrupting your shower."

"I'm just going to keep scrubbing. The hot water here doesn't last very long."

"Okay."

Jessica sat back up and tried not to stare at Sacrifice, even though she couldn't make out anything unseemly in the smoke. "Hey, uh…" asked Jessica, looking at the floor. "Can I ask you some questions anyway?"

"No."

"Yeah. Sorry. Yeah."

CHAPTER FOUR

The Bloodfist Underground

"Care to make a wager?" asked a scruffy looking wizard wearing an old, patched cloak. Floating just above his hands were a pair of magical gambling cubes, slowly whirring around each other.

"No," said Jessica, surveying the alley. She had come to the seediest corner of Bloodfist City, the last corner left where dark wizards could practice their craft without worry of interference by the authorities.

"Just five wizard coins to play. Guess which cube binds the soul of an ancient blood demon and win *fifty* coins!" The cubes both began shaking and emitting an eerie yellow light.

Jessica pulled out a small, orange coin sack. "I'll give you five coins for anything helpful you can tell me about Sacrifice."

The cubes stopped shaking, and the yellow light faded. The old wizard put both cubes into a large pocket in his cloak. "You're looking for Sacrifice, are you? You're with the Bloodfist Wizard Council then, I suppose?"

The Bloodfist Wizard Council was the local government, and had ultimate authority over the city. In the wizard realm there was no central governing body, just a mostly-cooperative network of municipal governments and alliances.

Jessica wondered for a moment if she should lie about her affiliation. "No, I'm… I don't want to tell you who I work for, I'm doing an investigation and I feel like that would be bad investigation protocol. But I don't work for the government."

"Oh. That's very honest and direct of you," said the old wizard.

"I'm new to investigating. I don't know if honesty is the best option but it feels weird to lie to you. I don't even know you."

The old wizard paused for a moment. "I was trying to scam you with the cubes."

"I know," said Jessica.

"Yeah, I figured you knew. But I didn't want to keep lying, it feels weird now."

"Sorry." The conversation had gotten less tense, but more awkward.

The old wizard looked around nervously. "Look, Sacrifice is a bad wizard, and I'm sure you have good reason to investigate her, but… there are thing going on in Bloodfist. Bad things, by wizards way worse than her."

Jessica was suddenly aware of the fact that she didn't know the first thing about what was going on in Bloodfist. She had only lived here a week, and only moved to the city because of the job offer. What exactly had she stumbled into the middle of? Jessica looked at the old wizard, and with a worried expression said, "Well, I hope I don't mess things up for everyone! I really hope that's not what I do!"

The old wizard considered her for a moment. "You should go to The Iron Claw. It's a claw shop. They sell all sorts of claws there. Tell them you're looking for a jade vulture claw."

"Is that a secret code?"

"Yes, obviously it's a secret code."

"Nice." Jessica gave the old wizard an awkward, knowing wink, thanked him, and handed him five wizard coins.

* * *

The Iron Claw looked even more run-down than the extremely run-down street it was located on. The capital letters on the store's sign had long since fallen off, and it now read, "HE RON LAW." There was a scorched hole in the wall next to the store's front door, and Jessica thought it looked a lot like a wizard inside had tried to shoot a fireball at someone as they left.

As she opened the shop door, Jessica was hit with an intense and unmistakable smell: birthday cake. It was the most birthday cake smelling smell she had ever smelled. It was so strong that she could taste it in her mouth, and feel it on her skin. Birthday cake. Every breath of air was birthday cake. Every second of existence was birthday cake.

A short, stout woman in dark brown coveralls walked up to Jessica and grabbed her hand, leading her in. "Sorry about the birthday cake smell, you'll get used to it in a minute, you just need to start walking."

Jessica followed the woman, trying to breath normally as the smell of birthday cake overloaded her senses. The shop looked nicer on the inside—the building itself was in disrepair, but everything else was clean and organized. The walls were lined with locked display cases filled with claws of every imaginable size and color. Small, printed placards below each claw gave a description, a list of common and uncommon uses, and a price.

"My name's Trex," said the woman as they reached the middle of the shop. She let go of Jessica's hand and motioned to the display cases. "We got all sorts of claws here, as you can see. Some of them are cursed and smell like an absolute nightmare, which is why there's a birthday cake charm on the shop. Sorry that it's a bit intense, but nothing else seems to overwhelm the other claw smells."

The smell of birthday cake was beginning to feel less oppressive, and Jessica was finding herself able to think again. "Wow. Yeah that's… a really intense smell charm. Yes. Yeesss."

"So, I assume you are in need of some sort of magical claw, then?"

"I am. I mean, okay… so I feel silly asking for this because it's not really a claw, it's a password, or secret code or something. Jade vulture claw? Does that make sense to you?"

"Ah." Trex looked disappointed. "You've been talking to ol' Two-Cubes Jackson."

Jessica stared blankly at the woman. "His name is Two-Cubes Jackson?"

"Yeah, on account of those two cubes he's got."

Jessica continued her blank, dull stare. "What if... what if he lost one of the cubes?"

"Never happened before."

"But what if it did happen?"

"He would just get another cube, I suppose. Or change his name."

Jessica felt a burning urge to go back to Two-Cubes Jackson and ask him various questions about his name, but she knew that would be extremely rude. "Anyway, jade vulture claw."

"Yup, heard you the first time." Trex turned around and left the room through a large hole in the back of the shop. A minute later she re-emerged, holding a small felt bag. "That'll be three wizard coins."

"What's in the bag?" asked Jessica.

"A jade vulture claw," replied Trex, annoyed.

"Oh. Yeah. What do I do with it?"

"There's a card in the bag. Three wizard coins. You look like you can afford it."

Jessica handed Trex three coins, and then opened the bag. Inside was a small jade vulture claw, and a card that read, "FOR USE WITH JADE VULTURES."

"Thanks buddy, that's a big help," said Jessica, rudely.

Trex turned around and walked back into the hole. As she disappeared into the darkness, she yelled, "I really don't care about any of this, I just want to sell claws!"

CHAPTER FIVE

A Wizardly Confrontation

It was the weekend, and the offices of Magical Investments were mostly empty. Jessica had decided to get caught up on her investment work, and was typing away on her magical calculator as it slowly tried to inch its way off the desk.

The investigation of Sacrifice had taken up most of Jessica's time recently, and she was worried that her investment portfolios were suffering for it. Of course, none of that mattered if the money she was managing remained stolen.

"Oh, dang it." Jessica realized that she was going to have to re-do the last ten minutes of calculations because of an earlier rounding error. She slid down her chair and sighed, and the calculator took the opportunity to completely fall off the desk and begin making its way over to a floor lamp across the room.

"Open up," commanded a voice from outside the door.

Jessica sat up, startled. Who was even at the office today? "Uh, come in!"

She waved her hand to open the door. Right at that very moment a cylindrical blob of wizard noodles appeared directly over where she was sitting, and slopped down forcefully onto her head. Cold, slimy noodles and salty broth ran down her face and robe.

The door opened and in walked Sacrifice, wearing gold starburst sunglasses and a tuxedo made from what looked like dinosaur skin. Under her arm was a huge rolled up poster of some sort, wrapped in a green and black ribbon, and hanging from her neck was the pendant Jessica had seen in her company portrait.

The surprise of seeing Sacrifice made Jessica momentarily forget about the surprise of the noodles. She jumped up from her chair to greet her, causing most of the noodles to slide off her face and onto the floor.

Sacrifice looked calmly at Jessica and said, "Sorry, were you in the middle of something?"

"Oh. No, I forgot to finish my wizard noodles a few days ago, and uh... here they are!" Jessica motioned unhelpfully at the noodles.

Sacrifice removed her starburst shades and stuck them into her jacket pocket, then began walking around the room, examining the placement of things. There wasn't much to examine—Jessica had not yet decorated the office, nor had she moved much around.

Sacrifice was about to say something when the floor lamp nearest her flickered and fell over. In landed with a smash, and glass from the bulb scattered across the floor.

Jessica's magical calculator scurried away from the scene, seemingly satisfied.

"It's the weekend, woo!" yelled Jessica, throwing her arms in the air.

For a second it looked like Sacrifice was amused, but only for a second. "After your call I thought I should look you up. See why you were showing up in my shower."

Jessica put her arms down. "Yeah, that was weird. Sorry about that, again."

"I couldn't believe it when I found out you work *here!* Right here at this company I'm all *executive* at!"

Jessica didn't like feeling deceptive, and this conversation was making her feel super deceptive. "Sacrifice, did you steal all the wizard gold? Like, the entire pile of wizard gold that's kept here?"

For the first time since she entered the room, Sacrifice looked surprised. "Uh, you can't just *ask* me if I stole the wizard gold."

"I can't? Is that a company rule, or am I breaking some sort of wizard etiquette?"

"I don't give two cubes about *etiquette!* But you can't…" Sacrifice paused for a moment, seemingly thinking deeply about something. "Are you a dark wizard, or a wizard of the light?"

"Neither, I guess. I've done some… dark things, but like, I don't actually care about darkness that much."

"Hmm. Okay, see, the wizards who come after me are usually wizards of the light, and there's this whole routine we go through." Sacrifice's stance softened a bit.

"I'm not… coming after you, at least I don't think I am. I'm just trying to figure out what happened to the wizard gold." In that moment, Jessica couldn't help but notice how beautiful Sacrifice's eyes were in person—they were a deep, rich black with small bits of emerald green sprinkled throughout. She also noticed that the pendant around Sacrifice's neck had a small, jade vulture claw embedded in it.

"Do yourself a favor, don't go looking for the gold. You're not going to find it."

"What does the jade vulture claw do?" Jessica asked, pointing at the pendant.

Sacrifice looked surprised for a second time. It was not a natural look for her. She grabbed her pendant and stared aggressively at Jessica. "Why?"

Jessica clumsily went through her pockets and pulled out her own jade vulture claw, holding it up for Sacrifice to see. "I have one too, but I don't know what to do with it. The card it came with said it's for use with jade vultures, but that didn't really make any sense to me."

"*You* shouldn't have that. Who gave it to you?"

Jessica felt a tingling warmness inside her head, and quickly recognized that she was being put under some sort of spell. Assuming it to be a truth-telling enchantment, she made a brief flicking motion with her hand and summoned a white orb, which flashed brightly and then dissipated. The enchantment had been broken.

Sacrifice shot Jessica an annoyed look, and said "Do you even know what spell I was casting?"

"A... truth-telling enchantment?"

"Yes, but which enchantment? Because I was casting an *extremely rare one* and you shouldn't have been able to break it without knowing *exactly* what it was."

"I'm not good at a lot of things, but I'm really good at breaking enchantments."

Sacrifice began pacing, staring grumpily at Jessica.

"Look," said Jessica, "lying isn't really my plan here. You can talk to me like a regular wizard. There are some things I can't tell you, but I won't lie."

Sacrifice stopped pacing. She walked over to Jessica and placed the rolled up poster she was holding onto the desk. Jessica took a step back to give her room, but Sacrifice jerked forward and positioned herself directly in front of Jessica's face. Jessica tried to think of something clever or intimidating to say, but was distracted by how dazzling the eyes in front of her were. The room was dim because of the broken lamp, but the specks of green in Sacrifice's eyes had a glow about them that made them sparkle even in low light.

"Call me again sometime. You're not terrible," Sacrifice said, and then she turned on the spot and marched out of the room, waving the door shut herself.

Jessica exhaled intensely and put her hand on her chest. "Oh, yeah," she said, feeling the damp broth on her robe, "I'm covered in noodles."

She began wiping the remaining noodles off her body, and then remembered the rolled up poster that had been left on her desk. The ribbon was the same colors as Sacrifice's eyes, Jessica noticed. "Nice," she said to herself. "I wonder if that was intentional."

With a quick pull she removed the ribbon and the poster unfurled, revealing a huge photograph of Sacrifice playing electric bass.

CHAPTER SIX

Secrets of the Jade Vulture

It is a known fact that most wizards are extremely unimaginative name-givers. Wizard secret societies are often named in such a way that the "secret" purpose of the society is immediately obvious, such as the *Cabal of the Seven Seals,* which "secretly" seeks to discover and activate seven ancient seals. Or the *Cult of Grandor's Return,* which "secretly" seeks to summon the deceased dark wizard Grandor.

Wizard cities are much the same. Bloodfist City, for instance, got its name from the fact that when you look at the sun from within city limits it resembles a huge bloody fist, thanks to an old and largely benign curse.

It was because of this fact about wizard naming conventions that Jessica decided to walk around the city looking for literal jade vultures. It didn't take long to find one—in fact, there seemed to be huge jade vulture statues every few blocks, usually poorly hidden in alleyways or crammed next to dumpsters. There were so many of them, and they were so large and out of place, that Jessica was certain they had to be enchanted with some sort of spell that made them particularly unnoticeable. After all, she had spent more than a week in Bloodfist City and this was the first time she had seen them.

A short, middle-aged businessman was walking down the sidewalk toward Jessica, and so she decided to test her theory. "Excuse me, sir?" she asked.

"Yes?" The man seemed uncomfortable at the realization that he was about to be asked a question. Questions often spiral out of control when you're a wizard. Questions lead to impossible, unthinkable answers. Questions are dangerous.

"Do you see the huge jade vulture over there?" Jessica asked, pointing at a statue across the street.

"Uh, no, I..." The man paused for a moment. "Wow, look at that! Weird!"

"So you see it?"

"Wow! Wowza! Yes, there's a huge... big ol' jade bird over there! What? Ha ha, what!" The man was both confused and delighted by this discovery.

"So you haven't seen it before?"

"No, and I walk this way every day! Wow! Oh my god and there's another one over there! What? Ha ha, wow!" The man put his hand on his head in amazement. "What a city! Ha ha!" He walked away, laughing to himself and looking around for more vultures, of which there were many.

"Well, I guess the only thing left to do is claw at one of those big birds," Jessica said, and she walked over to a statue nestled between two dumpsters in a dirty alley. The statue was around five feet tall, and covered in a thin film of grime that dulled its green surface into a dark gray. It was well carved, and Jessica thought the vulture looked almost noble, despite all the filth. As she inspected the statue, she noticed that there was a number imprinted on the vulture's head: "47."

"Interesting," she said to herself, although she wasn't sure if it actually was interesting. "Very interesting."

The next thing she noticed was the missing claw on the vulture's left foot. "Ah, now this I'm *sure* is interesting," said Jessica, still not actually sure if it was interesting. She took out her own jade claw and held it up to the statue. It looked like it would fit perfectly in the missing claw spot.

Jessica hesitated. She knew that if she connected her jade vulture claw to the statue something magical would happen, and that magical something would lead her further along her current investigatory path, a path that she feared would end with her eating another beautiful, perfect, living whole horse. Was any of this worth the death of a majestic wonder-beast? She sighed deeply, thinking about the grim position she had been put in, and then placed her claw on the foot of the statue.

Jessica felt as though she had been dropped from a very great height, although by all accounts she had't moved an inch. She was still in the same alley, in front of the same jade vulture statue. But… the sound was wrong. Gone was the hustle of wizards heading home from work, and the distant chromatic chirping of magical birds at the park a few blocks down. Now all that could be heard was a thin, haunting wind sweeping across the city.

The color, Jessica soon decided, was also wrong, but only slightly. Everything had turned faintly, almost imperceptibly greener. Everything *smelled* greener too, but she couldn't tell if that was just her imagination.

She put the jade claw back into her pocket and left the alley. The street was exactly as it had been moments before, except now there were no cars, or wizards, or anything that moved.

"Hello?" yelled Jessica, looking around for a reaction. Her voice echoed back, faintly, and then all she could hear was the wind. She walked up the street, looking into shop windows for signs of movement, but there was no one around. Block after block she searched, her pace increasing, but she found nothing except empty streets and empty buildings. "Hellloooo?" she yelled again, her voice betraying a tinge of panic.

"Why are you yelling? Stop it," came a voice from behind Jessica.

Jessica was so surprised that she almost lost her balance, and when she turned around to respond all she could think to say was, "No *you* stop it!"

"Jeez," replied the voice, which Jessica could now see belonged to a hefty middle-aged woman with shoulder-length brown hair and extremely bushy eyebrows. "What a thing to say!"

Jessica felt both silly and confused, and wasn't sure how to alleviate either of those feelings. "Where is everyone?" she asked, trying to sound reasonable and in control.

"What? Who's everyone?" asked the woman, as if Jessica's question was absurd.

Jessica motioned her arm toward the empty street and asked, "All of the people, where are they?"

"Listen dear, if you have someone specific you're

looking for maybe I can point you in the right direction, but I don't…" The woman paused for a moment, and then her eyes narrowed. "Have you been here before?"

"I've… been on this street, yes, but not while it has been so empty."

"So, someone gave you one of those claws without explaining what it did, huh?" The woman threw her arms up. "Totally irresponsible! Just totally irresponsible! Why you probably thought the world had ended!"

"Yes, I did maybe perhaps think that."

The woman reached her hand out to Jessica. "I'm Wraith. Sorry you just went through such a scare."

Jessica shook Wraith's hand and said, "I'm Jessica. So where am I?"

"You're in the Jade Realm. Or the Vulture Realm, depending on who you're talking to. It's Bloodfist City, but hidden away from everyone else."

"Ah." Things were starting to make more sense to Jessica, but only a little.

"You know what? Follow me dear, I'll make you some tea and explain everything. This way!" Wraith scuttled off across the street, and Jessica hesitantly followed.

* * *

Wraith lived in a quaint little tea shop called Cup of Magic, which was a popular stop in Bloodfist City, but in the Jade Realm in was quiet and eerily bare. The shelves in the back were completely empty, and the tables and chairs were all missing. A mattress had been set up on one side of the room, and a cauldron hung above a small fire in the corner.

"I go to Bloodfist now and then to nab some tea from this place, so I hope you don't mind stolen tea," said Wraith, walking to the cauldron.

"That's fine, thank you," said Jessica, who was feeling excited about the thrill of drinking stolen tea, and also feeling dorky for finding that thrilling.

"Jasmine, Earl Grey, or mint?"

"I'll have some jasmine, thanks." Jessica looked around the shop, trying to make sense of things. "How long have you lived here?"

"Oh, it's been two or three years I think, I was part of the first group sent over." Wraith dumped some tea leaves into the cauldron and gave it a quick stir.

"How many people are there in the Jade Realm?"

"I'm not sure, a few thousand maybe? Most of them take their chances in Bloodfist during the day and only come here to sleep."

"I still don't understand *why* this place exists."

Wraith took out two cups, and began ladling tea into them. Her expression had turned very sour, and Jessica was worried that she had said something wrong.

"I'm sorry," said Jessica, "did I…"

"How long have you lived in Bloodfist?" Wraith asked, handing a cup over to Jessica. The smell of jasmine was mellow and calming.

"Just a little over a week."

"I'm not going to give you the whole sad story, but a few years ago the Bloodfist Wizard Council decided it would be better for the *financial capital of the wizarding world* if there weren't so many *non-contributors* around.

Meaning wizards who couldn't work, or who had run into hard times." Wraith took a sip of her tea.

"So they sent you here?"

Wraith was looking even more sour. "They rounded people up, sent them off into the surrounding deserts. A lot of good wizards died. A few who didn't came back and set up the Jade Realm, and they've been hiding people here ever since."

Jessica was stunned. "The wizard council was sending people into the desert to die?"

"Still are. They call it the *Bloodfist City Relocation and Restoration Project.* It isn't even done in secret, that's what really gets me." Wraith looked like she was either about to cry or smash her cup.

Jessica looked awkwardly at the floor, not sure what to say.

"Enough about that," said Wraith, taking another sip of her tea. "Tell me, why did you come here, Jessica? Given how little you know about this place I'm assuming you aren't a rescue."

"Are you familiar with the dark wizard Sacrifice?"

Wraith gave a hearty laugh. "What a terror that one is. I don't have much good to say about Sacrifice except that she really seems to stick in the council's craw, so she can't be all bad."

"Does she come here, to the Jade Realm?"

"I see her flying around now and then, she's hard to miss. Some nights her band puts on a sort of musical light-show downtown. It's not very good but it ain't like there's much else to do here."

The sun was starting to set. They talked for a bit about

tea, and magic, and then Jessica thanked Wraith for her hospitality.

By the time Jessica made it back through the vulture statue to Bloodfist City, and then back to her apartment, it was almost midnight. She collapsed onto the pile of clothes on her bed and quickly fell asleep.

CHAPTER SEVEN

What One Wishes

Jessica wasn't very good at managing investment portfolios, but as luck would have it neither was anybody else, and so her incompetence had gone completely unnoticed. During her second week she realized that she could make choices entirely at random and end up with roughly the same results. This was a fortunate discovery, because she had lost all motivation to do her job properly.

After her visit to the Jade Realm, Jessica did extensive research into the city's Relocation and Restoration Project, and it was exactly as Wraith had described. The city was rounding up wizards who didn't meet the council's constantly fluctuating standards of acceptability and moving them into the neighboring deserts colloquially known as *"The Deathlands."*

Jessica wondered why there wasn't more outrage. The program had been active for years, and yet there didn't seem to be much political opposition. Did people even realize it was happening? And was the company Jessica worked for involved in any way? She decided that she had to confront Dr. Clash about it.

"Please, come in," said Dr. Clash as Jessica entered her office.

There was a bright glowing orb floating near the door that hadn't been there the last time Jessica had stopped by. It gave off a subtle, comforting heat, but somehow it didn't seem to actually shine any light upon the room around it.

Dr. Clash was finishing a cup of tea, and motioned to the tea pot. "Would you like a cup?"

"No," said Jessica, more coldly than she meant to.

Dr. Clash looked up from her tea. "Is something wrong?"

Jessica had imagined this conversation over and over again, but now that it was actually happening she found it difficult to begin. "Is... does Magical Investments..."

As she spoke, she noticed herself instinctively turning toward the luminous orb, unable to focus on what she was trying to say.

"Uh... what's up with the orb?"

"Oh, sorry, I forgot that you hadn't seen it. It's a wishing star. It doesn't actually grant wishes, but it makes you *believe* it can grant wishes."

"Yeah, I'm getting a really big wish-making impulse right now. So it doesn't work?"

"Nope. It just tries to get you to wish upon it. Once you know what's going on it's easy to resist. I find it funny, and this job can be boring, so, you know."

Jessica looked into the star, very much feeling like she should make a wish. "Yeah, it's pretty funny. And weird."

She turned away from the star and the impulse quickly faded.

"So, what were you saying?" asked Dr. Clash.

"Do you know about the Relocation and Restoration Project?"

Dr. Clash looked uncomfortable. She set her tea down on the desk and waved her hand, shutting the door behind Jessica. "That's... not a good thing to talk about in the open here."

"Is Magical Investments involved? Listen, I don't know if I can work for..."

"Hold on." Dr. Clash took a small bronze key from a chain around her neck, and put it into a keyhole on the bottom drawer of her desk. There was a quick metallic clinking sound, and the drawer popped open. It took a few moments for Dr. Clash to sort through the items in the drawer, but eventually she pulled out a small stack of papers and placed them neatly on the desk.

Jessica walked over and surveyed the papers, which looked like an assortment of memos and legal documents. "What are these?" she asked, placing her left hand on top of the stack.

"Evidence. Evidence that I hope to use one day, when the opportunity strikes. Take a look."

Jessica picked up the stack and began sifting through it. It was a collection of letters of opposition to the Relocation and Restoration Project, as well as opposition letters concerning other council projects that Jessica hadn't heard of. Attached to each letter was another document: a certificate of death regarding the letter writer.

"There were many of us in the wizard financial sector

who opposed the draconian measures the Bloodfist Wizard Council was taking," said Dr. Clash, solemnly. "Those who openly opposed the council's wishes were permanently removed from service." Dr. Clash was now looking out the window near her desk.

"They had all these people killed?" asked Jessica, carefully studying the documents.

"I believe so, but there was only ever circumstantial evidence to prove it. So I kept my mouth shut and began documenting everything I could." She paused for a moment, as if uncertain how to continue. "There's more."

Dr. Clash reached into the unlocked desk drawer and pulled out another document. It was a carefully plotted financial chart.

"There was one company that benefited from not just the council's policies, but also each of the deaths," said Dr. Clash. "Magical Investments."

"Whaaaaaat?" Jessica wasn't sure what else to say to such a startling revelation.

"It's how we ended up controlling half of all the wizard gold. So much of our competition was murdered right out of the market."

"But... you run this company," said Jessica, angrily.

"The board of directors runs it, I just manage the day-to-day operations. Take a look at those death certificates again, notice anything peculiar?"

Jessica looked through the death certificates, searching for anomalies. The wizard Urga the Incredible, CEO of Magic Money, had died during a botched attempt to turn her desk into an airplane. The wizard Tina Rex, board member of Wizardly Financials, had died misjudging the size of the room she was in while transforming into a dinosaur. The wizard Torn, president of Money Power, had died after accidentally turning himself into a bomb. "They all died in transmutation accidents. Each and every one of them," said Jessica.

"There are a number of board members here at Magical Investments who specialize in transmutation spells. I could never figure out which of them were behind the killings."

"Why do you still work for these people?"

"I thought I could do more to fight them from the inside. Collect evidence, bide my time. But I was wrong, they've been too good at covering their tracks. I don't even know if the Bloodfist Wizard Council was involved in the killings, or if they just never investigated because the murders all happened to benefit their agenda."

It was a lot for Jessica to take in. She had expected her time at Magical Investments to be simple, boring even. But two weeks into the job and she had found herself in the middle of a complex corruption, murder, and human rights scandal. After taking a minute to think about things, she looked up at Dr. Clash and asked, "Should I even keep investigating the robbery?"

"If that money isn't returned…" Dr. Clash began locking the documents back up in her desk. "These are dangerous wizards, who have been robbed of a great sum. If the money isn't found soon, well, I'm afraid of what they might do to get it back."

"Okay. I'll keep looking. Thank you, Dr. Clash, for being open to me about this. I understand what a dangerous position you've put yourself in." Jessica glanced over at the hovering star, and again felt an intense desire to wish into it. "Can I ask you one more thing?"

"Sure, go ahead."

"What do you feel yourself wanting to wish for when you look at the star?"

Dr. Clash looked nervous and embarrassed. "I, uh, that's a question I'm not going to answer, sorry."

"My wish is embarrassing too. When I look at the star I find myself unable to think about anything except eating another horse."

"You want to eat another horse more than *anything else in the world?*"

Jessica looked at the floor, paused for a moment, and then looked directly and intensely into Dr. Clash's eyes and said, "You shared dangerous information about yourself with me, I guess I can repay the favor."

Dr. Clash sat down on the edge of her desk, ready to listen.

"I have a hunger. It's always there, binding itself to my thoughts, my words... I try to suppress it, but it is a part of me and always has been. I hunger for power. I hunger for strength. For strength over others. It is not an aspect of myself that I am proud of. I've hurt people, and I've felt good doing it."

Dr. Clash shifted slightly, but if she was feeling any judgement about what Jessica was saying her face wasn't showing it.

Jessica continued staring into Dr. Clash's eyes, unblinking, and said, "When I was younger I heard stories of wizards consuming the bodies of other wizards to absorb their power. The idea of gaining so much strength, so quickly… it was an intoxicating thought. But I did not simply desire to posses the power of wizards. I wanted to obtain a power greater than any wizard had *ever* possessed. I wanted to posses the power of nature's greatest, most extraordinary, most vital miracle: the horse."

Small beads of sweat were forming on Dr. Clash's forehead.

"I knew that to absorb the full power of a horse I needed to do more than simply consume its flesh. I needed to consume the entire horse as one whole, complete being, and make it a part of myself. So, I researched absorption spells, and ancient abandoned magic involving the merging of two beings into one. I came to realize that to fully and completely make the horse a part of myself, a simple spell would not be adequate. No, I would need to permanently alter my very being. Change myself so that I was no longer human. I would still look human, but underneath I would be something different, a creature, a soul capable of opening itself up and swallowing a horse whole, making it a part of me forever."

Dr. Clash nodded, and a small drip of sweat fell from her face.

For the first time since she began the story, Jessica looked away from Dr. Clash, looking instead at the hovering star. "I became a monster, make no mistake. The process worked, you see, and I consumed a horse completely and fully. It is still a part of me, it is still a part of my power. But I was not satisfied, and that frightened me more than anything ever has. I had the perfect power of a horse within me, and it wasn't enough. I was afraid of what I might eventually do to quench my thirst for strength, and so I altered myself again, removing my ability to consume other beings. But it was too late. I discovered that although I could no longer consume animals or wizards, I could still consume horses, because I had already absorbed a horse into my soul. And so I did it again. I absorbed a second horse, giving me the combined power of two magnificent equine beasts."

Jessica looked back into Dr. Clash's eyes.

"I've been running from that version of myself ever since. Running from my lust for more power, more horses. But even with all that running, when I look at your star that's still what I want. I want to consume an entire, fully grown beautiful adult horse in one huge bite."

Jessica's eyes began to water. This was the first time she had ever told this to anyone.

Dr. Clash stood up from the desk, walked over to Jessica, and embraced her warmly. Then she turned her head toward Jessica's ear and said, "This is all very confusing, but thank you for telling me. That was very brave."

Jessica didn't feel brave. There were two murdered horses galloping around in her soul, and she wanted more.

CHAPTER EIGHT

Blob Life

A large, sticky, translucent blob lay motionless on the floor of Jessica's apartment. It had been there all day, completely inert outside of a slow, oozing expansion as it settled into the grooves in the floor.

The apartment was a mess. Jessica's clothes were no longer simply piled on the bed, they were also strewn across the counters and stuffed lazily into the cupboards. Cups of half-eaten wizard noodles were splattered on the floor and walls, giving the room an unpleasant brothy smell. The only thing moving in the apartment was a confused fruit bat, who was squeaking and flapping her wings dramatically as she flew around the ceiling looking for a way out.

As the squeaking of the bat grew louder, the translucent blob began to pull itself together and solidify. Within a minute it had ceased being a translucent blob, and was instead a completely opaque Jessica.

"Alright, hold on *bat,*" said Jessica, groggily, as she

stumbled over to the apartment's only window, which was still blocked by her moving boxes.

The bat's squeaks grew louder and angrier. Jessica impatiently knocked a stack of boxes to the floor, revealing the apartment's window and its gloomy view of Bloodfist City.

It took a moment for Jessica to get the window unlatched and open, but as soon as she did the bat swooped out of the opening and flew far away from the apartment.

"Bye bat, I thought you would be a good pet, but I guess you need to live in a tree or something," said Jessica, and then she turned herself back into a translucent blob and splattered to the floor.

A few minutes passed, and then Jessica reformed again. "This blob form is making me even *more* depressed. Good one, Jessica." Jessica high-fived herself, and then sat against the wall.

She looked around her small apartment, but there wasn't much to see besides the mess. It had been a rough couple of days for her, having just learned that the city's government and her employer were part of a sinister murderous conspiracy. Not to mention her ongoing feelings of guilt and shame regarding her own sinister horse-eating.

"*Blaaaahhhhhhh...*" said Jessica, as she slowly tipped herself over so that the maximum amount of her body could be touching the floor and wall at once. As her torso hit the ground, she felt the crunch of rolled-up paper beneath it. "*Blaaaahhhhhhh...*" she said again, twice as loud, as she pulled the paper out from under her.

It was the poster Sacrifice had given her the previous week, now bent and wrinkled. Jessica unrolled it and looked at Sacrifice, who was holding a black and gold bass guitar and wearing a snake-print shirt, snake-print leggings, and a snake-print bandana. Somehow it wasn't too much snake-print, Jessica thought. It was exactly the coolest amount of snake-print.

"Sacrifice. *Saccriiifffiiiicccceeee...*" Jessica said to the poster. "Sacrifice, let's hang out. I want you to cradle me like a baby, Sacrifice." Jessica laughed at herself. "Sacrifice. Help me clean up my apartment and then cradle me like a tiny useless baby."

Jessica fell back to the floor, clutching the poster to her chest.

"Sacrifice, sing to me, sing me a song. Pick me up and throw me in the garbage, Sacrifice." Jessica laughed at herself again. "I'm trash, Sacrifice. I'm a trash baby, sing to me and throw me in the garbage."

Jessica put the poster on the ground and stared at the ceiling. For a few minutes she didn't move, lying completely motionless outside of an occasional inhale or exhale. Then, in a sudden burst of chaotic energy, she leapt off the ground, grabbed her purple bottle and red feather from one of the toppled boxes, dipped the feather into the bottle, and used it to write "Sacrifice, I want to talk" on the poster.

There was a terrible howling sound, and the poster burst into a purple flame. A white smoke emerged from the fire and rapidly formed itself into a vague image of Sacrifice.

"Ah, you called," said Sacrifice, who looked like she was in the middle of smashing something with a metal pipe. "I'm in the Jade Realm right now, if you want to hang out. The construction site off Firestorm Road."

"I'll be there in ten."

CHAPTER NINE

A Night of Sacrifice

The Jade Realm felt colder than Bloodfist City, thought Jessica as she walked down an empty street on her way to meet Sacrifice. Maybe it was the lack of people and vehicles, or maybe it was the constant thin breeze. It was hard to tell how many of the differences were simply her imagination.

The sun was just beginning to set as she arrived at the construction site. Huge steel scaffolds dotted the area, and raw materials lay in massive piles around the plot. The frame of the building had been completed already, and it looked to be at least twenty stories high. A flimsy chain link fence blocked off the site, covered in signs that read, "COMING SOON: SPELLBOUND BANK & TRUST." This was going to be an enormous bank, Jessica thought.

Sacrifice was nowhere to be seen, but from Jessica's viewpoint most of the area was obscured by either scaffolds or mounds of dirt. She jumped over the chain link fence and walked to the building frame itself, which was truly, absurdly large for a bank.

"Hello?" said Jessica, and then she shivered slightly and wrapped both her arms around her chest. Before leaving her apartment she had changed into her only truly stylish wizard robe—it was dark blue with a mandarin collar and rhinestone accents. But it was made of chiffon and didn't provide a lot of warmth, and as the sun faded behind the skyline the air was becoming downright chilly.

No one was there, and Jessica wasn't sure she wanted to wait around in the cold dark. Had Sacrifice left? Was there another construction site on this street? Maybe she could get a better look from the top of the building, she thought.

For a moment Jessica considered climbing the scaffolding, because it had been a long time since she climbed a good scaffold, but she doubted if her chiffon robe would survive the trip. A better option would be to enchant something with a levitation charm and ride it to the top. Jessica looked around for a suitable object, and decided on a jackhammer that was resting on the ground next to the building's foundation.

After a few failed attempts, one of which resulted in a second, slightly larger jackhammer appearing, Jessica finally managed to properly levitate the jackhammer in a way that looked safe enough to ride. She mounted it as one might a broom, and with a flick of her wrist she was slowly ascending into the air.

There were a few areas of magic in which Jessica was truly a master, but levitation charms almost never worked for her on the first attempt. She had hoped that consuming the power of horses would improve her wizarding skills all-around, but in practice it had only strengthened the things she was already good at.

And so, Jessica was ascending at a ludicrously slow speed as the jackhammer unsteadily wobbled its way up, inch by inch. Watching the last of the sunlight flicker away, and remembering that most of the Jade Realm's residents only came here at night, she was suddenly feeling very anxious about the possibility of being seen in such an awkward act of novice magic. Just as she was beginning to hear the distant murmur of wizards arriving in the realm, she reached the top of the building's frame.

"You made it," came a voice from off to the side.

Jessica got off the jackhammer and steadied herself on a metal beam. The jackhammer continued its ascent, slowly floating out of reach, and Jessica turned around to look where the voice had come from. Leaning casually against a scaffold and holding a large green bottle, wearing the studded leather jacket that Jessica had first seen her in, was Sacrifice.

"I was worried I was going to witness an exceptionally embarrassing death," said Sacrifice, grinning.

"Should I do something about that?" asked Jessica, pointing to the jackhammer, which was now five feet above her head.

"Don't worry about it. The way you charmed it, it's literally going to go up forever now."

"Oh. Okay, cool."

Jessica walked awkwardly along the beam over to Sacrifice, who held out her green bottle. Jessica grabbed it and took a swig. It tasted a lot like orange juice, tangy and sweet.

"What is this?" asked Jessica, who was now realizing the bottle didn't have a label.

"Magic juice. I made it myself. Gives you acute sensory perception for a few hours. Lots of fun."

"Whoa." Jessica's vision had suddenly come into extreme focus. Even though the sun had gone down, she could see all around her with an intense, bright clarity. The thin howl of the wind now sounded rich and detailed, and she could smell the remnants of a pleasant ginger perfume on Sacrifice's jacket.

"I like coming here. Bloodfist City's depressing," said Sacrifice, who grabbed the green bottle from Jessica and took a huge gulp.

Jessica watched as Sacrifice drank, taking in the beautiful and dramatic contours of her face, and the pleasing way her strong facial muscles moved beneath her skin. It was the clearest Jessica had ever seen a face, and what an incredible face it was. The specs of green in Sacrifice's eyes were glowing like peridot embers, and the beauty of it almost hurt.

"I think you're magnificent," said Jessica, feeling weird about her word choice almost immediately.

"Everyone does," said Sacrifice. "Everyone who isn't boring."

Sacrifice passed the bottle back to Jessica, who drank the last of the juice inside. The world sparkled in detail, and Jessica couldn't believe all of the shades of color she could see in even simple things, like her own chiffon robe.

Jessica set the bottle down on a metal beam, and Sacrifice kicked it with such force that it exploded into millions of tiny, shimmering particles.

"Whoooaaaaaaa…" said Jessica, watching as the bits of bottle floated away in a twinkly mist.

Sacrifice waved her hand in the air, and then turned to Jessica and asked, "Want to go somewhere neat?"

"Yes," Jessica said immediately. "I'll need some help getting down though."

"Yeah, I've got you."

There was a faint whirring sound, and then Sacrifice's gold and black bass guitar flew up like a bird of prey. Sacrifice grabbed it and jumped on—it was much more stable than Jessica's jackhammer had been.

"Hop on," said Sacrifice, looking nonsensically cool. Jessica unsteadily put her hands on Sacrifice's shoulders and then pulled herself onto the back of the bass.

In an instant they were flying forward, and Jessica clung tightly to Sacrifice for fear of falling. But the charm on the bass was perfect, and so even though they were traveling extremely quickly Jessica felt no momentum, and was never in any actual danger of falling.

As they sped over the empty rooftops of the Jade Realm, Jessica realized that for the first time in as long as she could remember she wasn't feeling either a deep desire to consume an entire horse, or a deeper guilt for the horses she had already absorbed. She felt *okay*, and for Jessica that was a miracle.

The bass began flying higher above the city, and soon they were high enough that the buildings below looked like tiny gray and brown stones. "Where are we going?" asked Jessica, watching the city disappear below her.

"We're almost there." Sacrifice pointed upward, toward a peculiar dark hole in the atmosphere above them.

"Cool," said Jessica, excited by how weird the night had been, and was continuing to be.

Passing through the hole in the sky felt like puncturing a very thin plastic barrier, and Jessica noticed an immediate change in temperature. The air in the Jade Realm had gotten quite frosty, but inside the hole there was a cozy warmth surrounding them.

Jessica's mouth dropped, and she loosened her grip on Sacrifice. They were now in a very charming, very grand log cabin. There was a fire roaring in a huge stone fireplace to their left, the flames swirling in impossible purples and blues. To their right was a massive cherry wood table covered in breads and fruits and dark red candles. The air smelled of fresh cut wood and orange blossom, and Jessica breathed it all in deeply.

"Well, this is my place," said Sacrifice, and she stepped off the bass. "Mind the hole."

Jessica looked down. There was a large hole beneath her, and through it she could see the distant buildings of the Jade Realm. "You live in a hole in the sky?" asked Jessica, impressed.

"Yeah. The Jade Realm's like a bubble, and I thought it would be cool to make a house on top of the bubble."

"You were right, it is cool. It's extremely very cool." Jessica stepped off the bass and walked around the cabin, taking in every detail with her juice-enhanced senses.

"Are you hungry?" asked Sacrifice, taking off her leather jacket, revealing a dapper black button-up shirt underneath.

"Yes," replied Jessica, in the sultriest voice she could muster. "Very."

Sacrifice slowly walked toward Jessica, setting her

jacket down on a large burgundy chair by the fireplace. "What would you like?"

They were now inches apart. Sacrifice's face was wild and beautiful in the firelight. Jessica leaned forward and said, "Let's start with this."

Their lips met, and they kissed with the combined passion of two wizards and two horses.

CHAPTER TEN

The Third Horse

Jessica's eyes slowly opened, squinting as they adjusted to the light. Daylight was streaming in through a nearby window, warming Jessica and giving the black satin sheets she was lying in a pleasant, shiny glow.

Sacrifice's bedroom was large and brashly decorated. A huge poster of herself hung on the far wall in an ornate golden frame. Beneath it was a table made of dark, twisted wood, covered in black and white roses. There was a dressing cabinet near the window, and one side of it had been left ajar, revealing a collection of very loud jackets and a few dangerous looking pants.

The door to the bedroom swung open and Sacrifice walked in, wearing a green and gray checkered morning robe and holding two large silver plates. "All I know how to make is pancakes, I hope that's okay."

"Yeah, gimme them cakes," said Jessica, grabbing one

of the plates. The pancakes were delicious, and Jessica gobbled them down like she hadn't eaten in days.

Sacrifice sat on the bed next to Jessica and stared out the window. There wasn't much to see from up here, but the light was warm and comforting.

"I did steal the wizard gold," said Sacrifice, her gaze still focused on the window.

Jessica stopped eating. In that moment she thought Sacrifice looked a lot like a wolf surveying a valley.

"I stole every last coin."

"Oh," said Jessica. "Why?"

"I hate this place. The city, the people, all of it. It's the money. Too much money, all in one place."

"Yeah." Jessica considered things for a moment, and then said, "You... destroyed it all, didn't you?"

Sacrifice looked toward Jessica, surprised. "How could you possibly know that?"

"It just seems like the sort of thing you'd do."

Sacrifice looked back out the window. "Yeah. I destroyed it. I thought about using it for something, but couldn't figure out a way to not screw up whatever I tried to help."

Jessica continued eating her pancakes. She was very hungry.

"My heart is black, Jessica. All I've ever been good at is destroying things. But it's never... it's never felt good until now."

Sacrifice looked at Jessica, a fierceness growing in her dark, green-speckled eyes.

"Destroying the money felt right, and nothing has ever felt right. You have to understand..."

"Yeah, no, I'm with you 100% on this," said Jessica, almost choking on a bit of pancake.

Sacrifice looked surprised. "What? Oh, my god, I thought you were going to hate me or something."

"No, I think taking and destroying all the money was the right call. The people you stole it from are *wacky* corrupt, and the corruption goes all the way to the government, so what else could you have done?"

Sacrifice flopped backward onto the bed. "Man, I worried all morning about telling you. But you're awesome, Jessica. I'm glad I made you pancakes. You deserve pancakes."

"Yes," said Jessica. "I do deserve pancakes." She continued eating. "So what are you going to do now? The company suspects you, and I imagine they'll find out for sure at some point."

"Maybe go to another city. Rob another firm. Light up some more wizard gold. I want that feeling again, the feeling that I'm doing something I was born to do."

"I think that's a good plan. And maybe…"

As Jessica said this, the room began to blur. Sacrifice jumped off the bed and looked at Jessica with fear and alarm.

"What's happening?" asked Jessica, dropping her plate of pancakes. Things were fading quicker and quicker.

"They're trying to grab *me*. They figured it out. I'm sorry Jessica, I'll…"

Everything went black, and there was a faint, unnatural hum. A few seconds went by, and then the humming stopped and the world started coming back into focus.

Jessica was no longer on Sacrifice's bed. Instead, she

was on the far end of a large, gray room, bound tightly to a large gray chair, at the head of a large gray desk. On the other side of the desk sat three sour-looking wizards that Jessica recognized as members of the Magical Investments board of directors.

The wizard on the left was a short, bearded man with wild red hair and thin, silver glasses. The wizard in the middle was a tall, sharply dressed woman with silver hair and a scar on her right cheek. The wizard on the right was a large, athletic-looking man with a shaved head and a missing right hand.

"Hey," said Jessica, not sure what else to do. "I'm Jessica, I work here."

The wizard in the middle very loudly and clearly said, "How interesting. We tried to grab Sacrifice from her bed, and instead we ended up with you."

"It's because we banged last night," said Jessica. "I'm supposed to report any interoffice romance, so this is me doing that."

The wizard on the right leaned forward, his face showing not a single tinge of emotion. "We are not going to kill you, as long as you tell us what we need to know. And we need to know where the gold is."

"It's all gone," said Jessica. "Completely destroyed."

The wizard on the left leaned forward, his face twisted in a foul, unnatural smirk. "Is that what Sacrifice told you? And you believed her?"

"Yes," replied Jessica.

"Sacrifice would not destroy so much wizard gold, no one would," said the wizard in the middle.

"Uh, you wouldn't, because you're all awful. And

she did, because she's not boring. You're all completely financially ruined," said Jessica, as sassily as she could muster given the stress of the situation.

The wizard in the middle cupped her hands together, and the wizards on the left and the right looked knowingly at each other. A few seconds passed, and the wizard in the middle stood up.

"Well, thank you for your service at our company. I am very sad to report that you were in a tragic transmutation accident today, dying in unimaginable pain on your way to work."

Jessica twirled her fingers around, and the magical restraints binding her to the chair disappeared.

The wizard on the left looked absolutely bewildered by this. "How did you…"

"Enchantment breaking, it's my main thing," said Jessica, backing away from the desk.

"Poor Jessica, a model employee, cut down so early in her career," taunted the wizard in the middle.

The other two wizards began muttering some sort of spell, but Jessica couldn't hear what they were saying.

"Jessica, who only worked here a few weeks, but whose memory will live on in our hearts forever," continued the middle wizard.

Jessica looked around frantically for a door. Realizing it might be enchanted, she waved her hands wildly in every direction until a large gray door appeared in front of her, its vanishing charm broken.

All three of the board members wizards were chanting in unison now, speaking the words of a spell that only a few people in the entire world would even recognize. But

Jessica recognized it, and knew the words well. It was an ancient, extremely dangerous merging spell. Running from the room, Jessica turned her head back for just a moment and saw the three terrible wizards fusing into one another, tendrils of flesh and blood and bone streaming from wizard to wizard until they had become one huge, awful entity.

Jessica panted and wheezed as she careened away from the room and down a huge, cavernous hallway, not daring to look behind her again. The hall was unimaginably large, and Jessica wasn't sure if there was even an end to it, but she knew that she had to keep running no matter what.

A wicked, terrible, poetic voice boomed violently from behind her and echoed off the hall's enormous stone walls. "Jessica, Jessica, poor, tragic Jessica..."

Jessica's legs were beginning to give out, but she forced herself forward.

"... dead, and we feel no remorse..."

Jessica wanted to scream but she didn't have the breath. Behind her she could feel enormous footsteps thundering closer and closer.

"... she was killed in this hall, after taking a fall..."

The floor below Jessica shifted, and she tumbled forcefully to the ground. The bones in her left arm snapped as she fell on it with the full weight of her body, and she let out a painful, breathless groan.

The thundering footsteps had arrived where she lay, and a huge, cold shadow fell upon her.

"... trampled to death, by a horse."

Jessica looked up at the source of the terrible, haunting voice. The three wizards had merged together and formed a gigantic, wraith-like horse.

There was a sudden silence in the hall. Jessica's eyes were gazing directly into the large, pearly black pupils of the wicked horse—but her gaze was no longer one of terror. It was a hungry gaze. A ravenous gaze.

The horse looked back in anger, offended by this change in her expression. Jessica could feel the souls of the three wizards swirling inside the form of the wicked beast. Dark, murderous, powerful souls, ready to take Jessica's life, ready to take anyone's life if it meant profit and fortune.

The horse slammed its hooves onto the ground irately, cracking the stone floor and shaking the walls, but Jessica sat motionless, eyes still fixed, her hunger growing. The horse bellowed a terrible roar that blew out the windows in the great hall, showering glass down like rain, but Jessica remained steady.

The horse lowered itself, and with all of its strength and might it lunged at her, its black eyes burning with hatred, its mouth open, salivating, ready to rip the flesh off Jessica's insolent face.

Then, something very strange happened. The shape of the room was changing, though the dreadful horse couldn't tell how. It was as if the very concepts of space and mass had been altered. Jessica's mouth had opened, and although it didn't seem to be open any wider than as if she were yawning, it somehow felt wider than the entire room. The horse tried to stop, to turn, but it was falling further and further toward the mouth, further and further away from the world.

The lips of Jessica's mouth began to close, and the horse felt itself being unmade. The tangle of wizards inside were being torn apart, piece by piece, and taken away to a place they would never see or understand. Jessica's lips closed together tight, and the terrible horse was no more.

CHAPTER ELEVEN

The Three Horse Wizard

There was a snapping sound, and suddenly Jessica was awake, confused and disorientated. She tried to get up, but something was keeping her from moving.

"Sorry," came a familiar voice. "One second. Try not to move."

Jessica's eyes were having a hard time focusing, and she was trying desperately to remember where she was or how she got there.

"Okay, you can sit up now."

Jessica sat up, and her vision slowly unfogged. She was in Dr. Clash's office, on the fainting couch, with Dr. Clash sitting next to her.

"I just set your arm. It'll be sore for a few days, but other than that you should be fine," said Dr. Clash.

"How did I…" Jessica began to ask.

"I heard a commotion in the board room. No one was

there, but I found you unconscious in the Infinity Hall, so I brought you here."

Jessica felt her arm. Most of the pain had faded.

"I am actually a medical doctor, it's not just a name. I originally went to school for magical healing," said Dr. Clash.

"Thank you." Jessica's memories were coming back, and she wasn't sure how she felt about them.

"So, what exactly happened? If you feel up to talking about it, that is."

"I…" Jessica put her right hand up to her mouth, as if to make sure it was still there. "I ate another horse."

"Oh, wow," said Dr. Clash, not sure how she should be reacting to this news.

"It was a magic horse, a fusion of three of the board members. They were the ones behind the killings."

Jessica explained what had happened, and pointed out the offending wizards on a company photo Dr. Clash had in her desk.

"And the money's all gone?" asked Dr. Clash.

"Yeah. That's what Sacrifice told me, and I believe her. Keeping the money would be a boring thing to do, and she is extremely not boring."

"Well, I guess my time as president is over." Dr. Clash walked over to her tea set and started preparing some oolong.

"I'm sorry," said Jessica. She felt bad about causing so much trouble for Dr. Clash, even though she was happy to see a corrupt company fall apart.

"Don't be. I've been done with this job for years, and

now that the killers have been, uh, eaten, I can move on to other things."

Jessica looked over at the luminous star hovering by the door. "Like the things you want to wish for with your star?"

"Hah!" Dr. Clash poured them both some tea. "One day I'll tell you what I feel when I look at the wishing star. But not today. So you've got to keep in touch if you ever want to find out."

"Deal," said Jessica. "What about the Bloodfist Wizard Council, and the Relocation and Restoration Project?"

"I suspect there's going to be a lot of eyes on the city once people realize half their money is gone. And I'm going to send those eyes a copy of the folder in my desk. If nothing comes of that, maybe I'll apply for a government position!"

Jessica took a cup of oolong from Dr. Clash, and sniffed it deeply. Oolong teas were Jessica's favorite.

* * *

It took over an hour for Jessica to float all the way up to the hole in the Jade Realm's sky, riding on a shopping cart she had improperly charmed. The hardest part ended up being getting through the hole itself—apparently it took more than just a gentle, slow push to break the barrier that separated the cabin from the rest of the realm.

The fire in the stone fireplace was no longer burning, and the candles had been blown out, but other than that the cabin appeared to be unchanged from the night before. Jessica searched from room to room for Sacrifice, but she was no longer there, and it didn't look like she would be coming back—her dressing cabinet had been completely emptied. Not a single jacket or studded belt remained.

Jessica gazed up at the huge portrait of Sacrifice that hung in the bedroom. It was a great portrait, Jessica thought. It truly made Sacrifice look like a huge, cool jerk.

"I could take it," said Jessica, surveying the frame, looking at how it was attached to the wall. "I could use it to call her up. I could do it."

Jessica sighed, and then grabbed one of the black roses from the table under the portrait, and headed home.

* * *

Everything was packed, which had been an easy task because Jessica had never actually unpacked, so getting her stuff ready to move again only took a couple of minutes. She was out of a job, and the city was on the verge of financial collapse. Therefore, it was time to go.

Usually when she left a city she left it with a sense of shame for the past, and dread for the future, but this time things were different. She had eaten a third horse and actually felt good about it, because it had been an evil horse made up of three immensely evil wizards. It was the coolest thing she had ever done, and it was the first time she felt like she deserved the power she had stolen.

Jessica looked around her small apartment one last time, taking in every detail. What a dull room, she thought.

As she opened the door to leave, a huge rolled-up poster fell into the apartment, bound with a black and green ribbon. Gasping, Jessica scooped it up in her arms, and impatiently ripped the ribbon away. The heavy poster unraveled, and as it did Jessica could smell cut wood and orange blossom. It was the portrait of Sacrifice from the cabin, with a note written in neon green ink on the bottom: "You forgot this, nerd. Call me. -S"

Made in the USA
Middletown, DE
04 December 2022

17056967R00043